THE FISH
The Story of the Stickleback

To Elaine M.L.

To Joanna and Lucy J.B.

Text copyright © 1981 by Margaret Lane
Pictures copyright © 1981 by John Butler
All rights reserved.
Library of Congress Catalog Card Number: 81-5545
Printed in Italy.
First Pied Piper Printing 1983
A Pied Piper Book is a registered trademark of The Dial Press.
First published in Great Britain in 1981 by Methuen/Walker Books
as *The Stickleback*

THE FISH: THE STORY OF THE STICKLEBACK
is published in a hardcover edition by The Dial Press,
1 Dag Hammarskjold Plaza, New York, New York 10017.
ISBN 0-8037-2603-1

THE FISH

The Story of the Stickleback

By Margaret Lane

Pictures by
John Butler

THE DIAL PRESS/New York

Sticklebacks are fish that live in fresh and salt water, in ponds, streams, and shallow inlets. They get their name from the three sharp spines on their backs. Full-grown sticklebacks are about two inches long, and for most of the year they are greenish black with silvery sides. With luck they may live as long as two years.

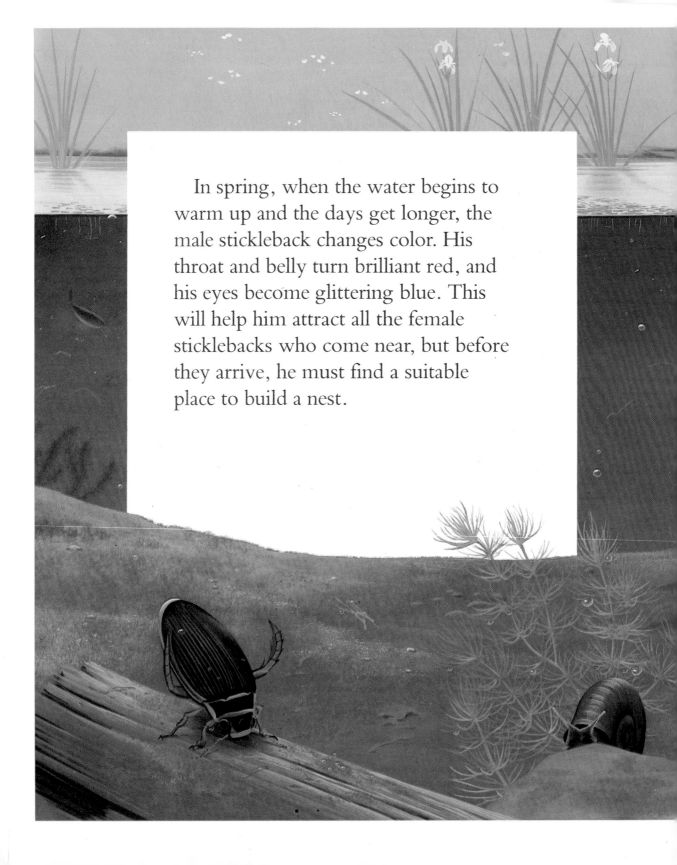

In spring, when the water begins to warm up and the days get longer, the male stickleback changes color. His throat and belly turn brilliant red, and his eyes become glittering blue. This will help him attract all the female sticklebacks who come near, but before they arrive, he must find a suitable place to build a nest.

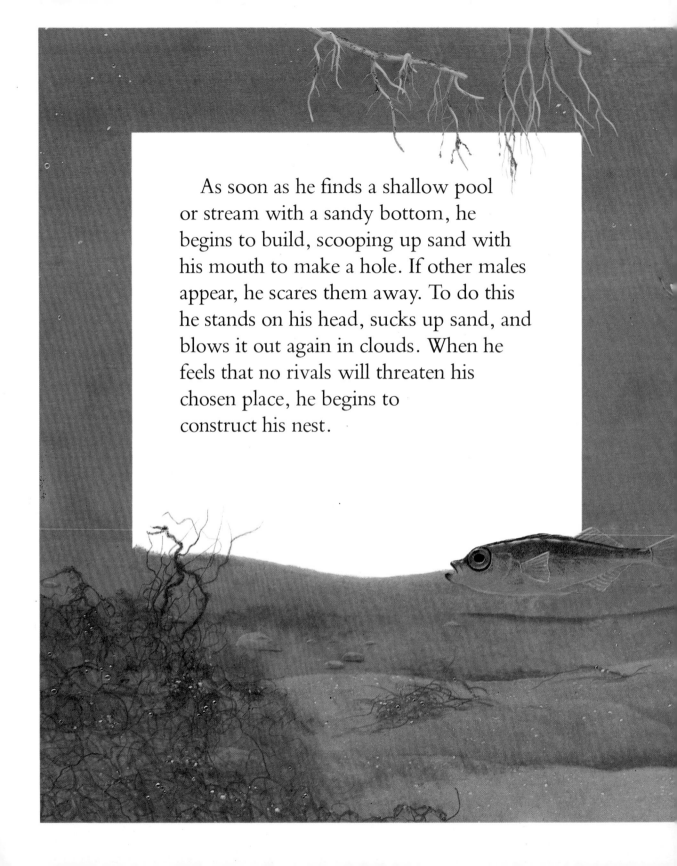

As soon as he finds a shallow pool
or stream with a sandy bottom, he
begins to build, scooping up sand with
his mouth to make a hole. If other males
appear, he scares them away. To do this
he stands on his head, sucks up sand, and
blows it out again in clouds. When he
feels that no rivals will threaten his
chosen place, he begins to
construct his nest.

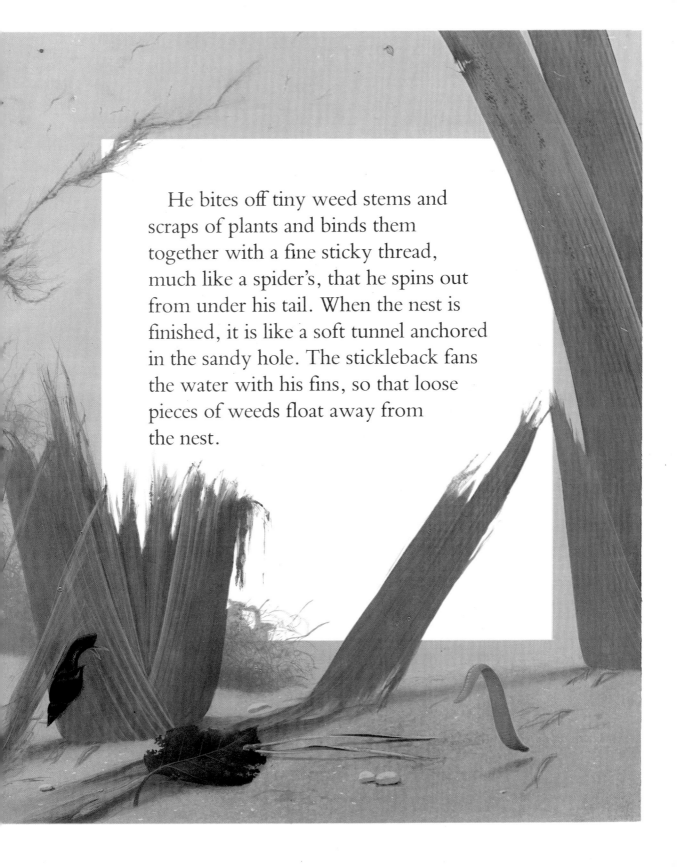

He bites off tiny weed stems and
scraps of plants and binds them
together with a fine sticky thread,
much like a spider's, that he spins out
from under his tail. When the nest is
finished, it is like a soft tunnel anchored
in the sandy hole. The stickleback fans
the water with his fins, so that loose
pieces of weeds float away from
the nest.

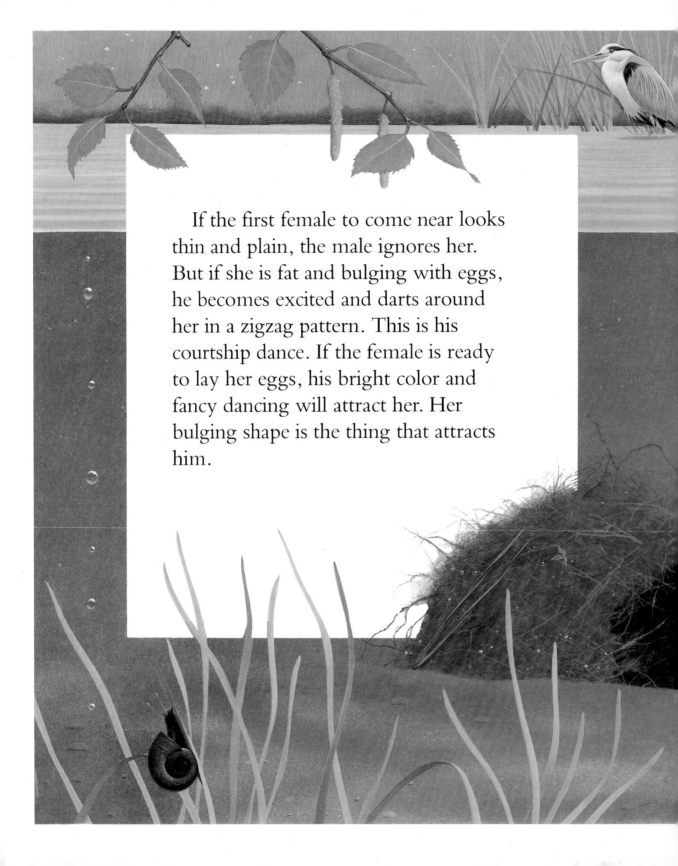

If the first female to come near looks thin and plain, the male ignores her. But if she is fat and bulging with eggs, he becomes excited and darts around her in a zigzag pattern. This is his courtship dance. If the female is ready to lay her eggs, his bright color and fancy dancing will attract her. Her bulging shape is the thing that attracts him.

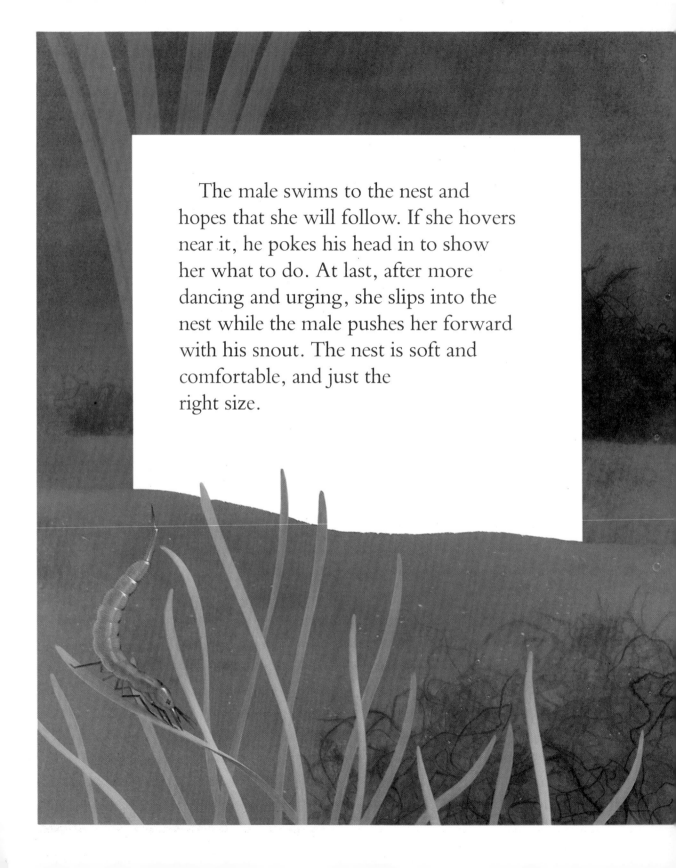

The male swims to the nest and hopes that she will follow. If she hovers near it, he pokes his head in to show her what to do. At last, after more dancing and urging, she slips into the nest while the male pushes her forward with his snout. The nest is soft and comfortable, and just the right size.

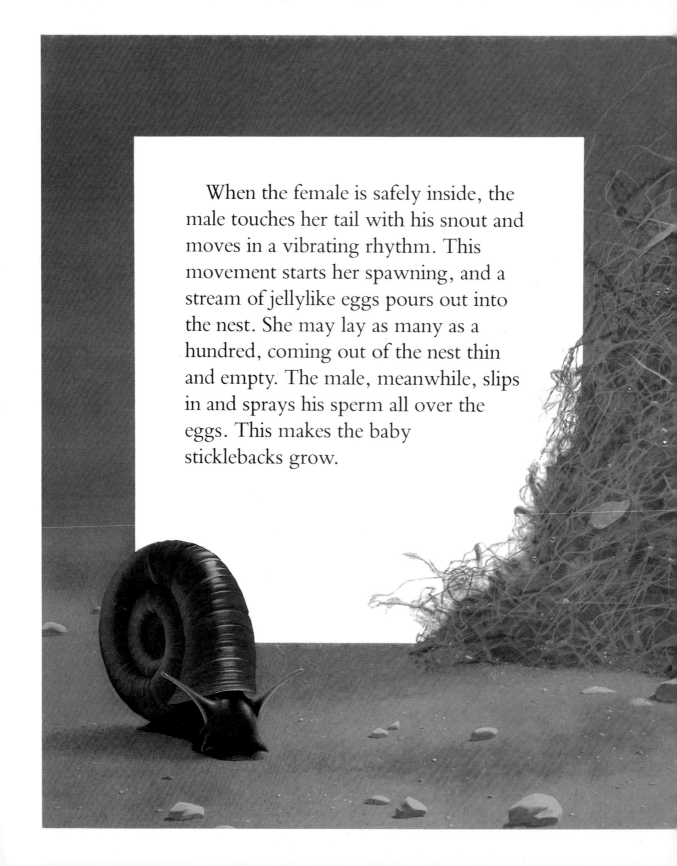

When the female is safely inside, the male touches her tail with his snout and moves in a vibrating rhythm. This movement starts her spawning, and a stream of jellylike eggs pours out into the nest. She may lay as many as a hundred, coming out of the nest thin and empty. The male, meanwhile, slips in and sprays his sperm all over the eggs. This makes the baby sticklebacks grow.

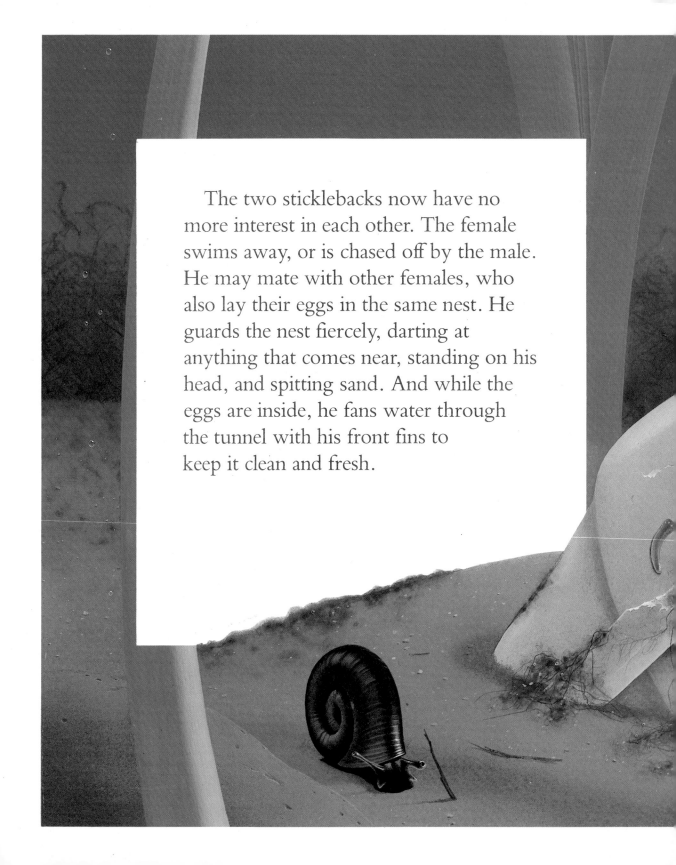

The two sticklebacks now have no more interest in each other. The female swims away, or is chased off by the male. He may mate with other females, who also lay their eggs in the same nest. He guards the nest fiercely, darting at anything that comes near, standing on his head, and spitting sand. And while the eggs are inside, he fans water through the tunnel with his front fins to keep it clean and fresh.

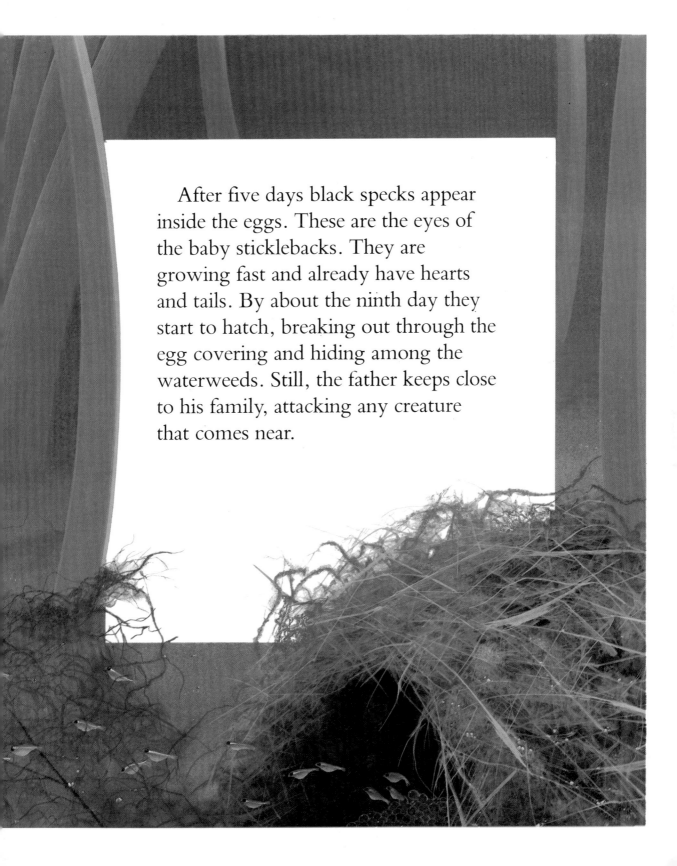

After five days black specks appear inside the eggs. These are the eyes of the baby sticklebacks. They are growing fast and already have hearts and tails. By about the ninth day they start to hatch, breaking out through the egg covering and hiding among the waterweeds. Still, the father keeps close to his family, attacking any creature that comes near.

If he did not guard them, few would survive. Young sticklebacks make a tasty meal for many hungry fish, birds, and other creatures. But when they are about two weeks old, the father stops caring for them and they have to take care of themselves, hunting water fleas and tiny worms. Meanwhile he will look for new mates and raise more broods. With luck he will have four or five families in a season.

When the last brood of the year is doing well, the male stickleback loses his bright color and is once more greenish black, like the female, with shadowy stripes on his back. Now bigger fish or birds will have difficulty spotting him and he is much safer from attack. The three sharp spines on his back are a good defense, too, making him painful to swallow.

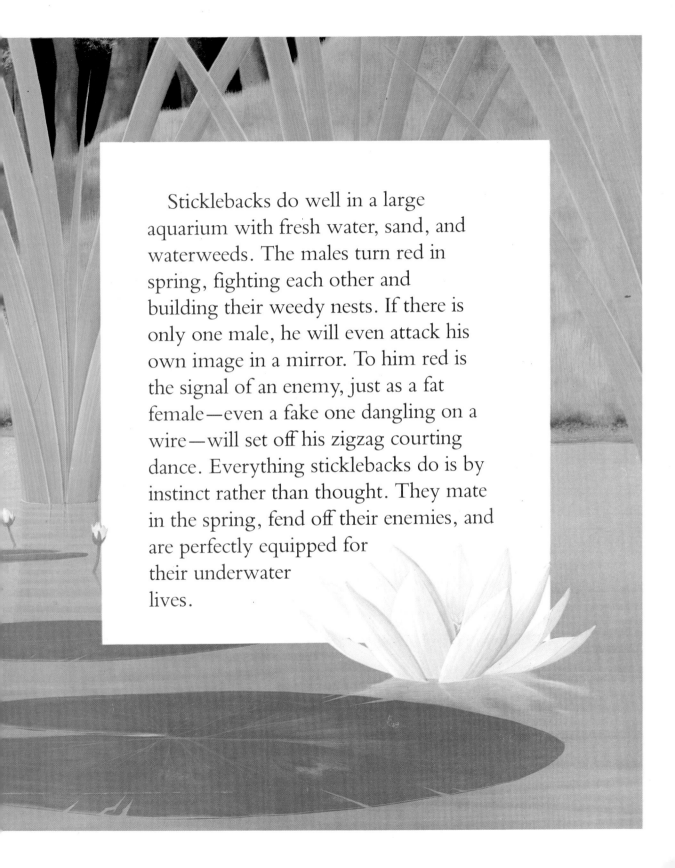

Sticklebacks do well in a large aquarium with fresh water, sand, and waterweeds. The males turn red in spring, fighting each other and building their weedy nests. If there is only one male, he will even attack his own image in a mirror. To him red is the signal of an enemy, just as a fat female—even a fake one dangling on a wire—will set off his zigzag courting dance. Everything sticklebacks do is by instinct rather than thought. They mate in the spring, fend off their enemies, and are perfectly equipped for their underwater lives.

About the Author

Margaret Lane is the celebrated author of outstanding books of fiction and biography, including *A Night at Sea, A Smell of Burning,* and *The Magic Life of Beatrix Potter.* Her most recent books for young readers are *The Frog* and *The Squirrel* (both Dial). She has worked as a journalist in London and New York and has written reviews for numerous literary publications.

Ms. Lane was educated at St. Stephen's College in Folkestone, England, and St. Hugh's College, Oxford. She lives with her husband, the 15th Earl of Huntingdon, in Beaulieu, England.

About the Artist

John Butler is a prominent artist and illustrator of wildlife. His paintings have been exhibited in numerous galleries and were included in a major exhibition to aid the World Wildlife Fund.

Mr. Butler lives in Tunbridge Wells, England, with his wife and two children.